Little Jimmy
and the Spoiled
Rotten Banana

Proverbial Kids©
Wisdom for Young Families

**Written and Illustrated by
Karen Anderson Holcomb**

WestBow Press books may be ordered through booksellers or by contacting:

WestBow Press
A Division of Thomas Nelson & Zondervan
1663 Liberty Drive
Bloomington, IN 47403
www.westbowpress.com
1 (866) 928-1240

ISBN: 978-1-5127-9900-2 (sc)
ISBN: 978-1-5127-9901-9 (e)

Library of Congress Control Number: 2017912301

Print information available on the last page.

WestBow Press rev. date: 07/24/2019

WestBow
PRESS®
A DIVISION OF THOMAS NELSON
& ZONDERVAN

Dedicated to my parents, Neil and Dianne Anderson, who trained my sisters and me in the way of the Lord; and to our Heavenly Father, who directs our paths as we trust in Him.

And Jesus increased in wisdom and stature, and in favor with God and men.

Luke 2:52

Little Jimmy was a boy who learned at a very early age how to always get what he wanted.

One afternoon Jimmy was very hungry. His Mama offered him a banana, but he wanted a piece of candy instead. He decided to show her just how upset he was.

"Wa-a-a," he cried. "Wa-a-a!"

This disturbed his Mama. Jimmy was only two years old. He was a precious boy, but her precious baby boy did not want a banana. He wanted candy.

So, she smiled and let him have it.

That was easy, Little Jimmy thought. He was a smart two-year-old, and he loved sweets.

He also loved French fries, soft drinks, and swirly blue cotton candy a whole lot more than carrots, milk, and broccoli.

All it took was a little fussing to get what he wanted.

"Wa-a-a!" he cried. "No!" he pouted.

By the time Little Jimmy was three years old, he could cry and say "no" as fast as he could wink. But his mother had forgotten how to say "no." She just said "yes" all the time. It was easier.

"Yes, you may have another piece of candy."

"Yes, you may climb on the piano."

His father had a hard time saying "no" as well.

"Yes, you may stay up until eleven o'clock."

"Yes, you may sleep with your pacifier—between your mother and me— in your hard hat."

When Jimmy was six years old, he asked for a smart phone, and he expected to get it.

"No," his mother said. "That wouldn't be good for you."

Little Jimmy got really upset.

He cried, and he shouted, "You don't love me!"

However, that was not true. Not every child had a smart phone, and his mother certainly did love him.

Still, he cried and cried like a two-year-old until ...

...his parents bought him one.

You see, Jimmy had his parents wrapped around his little finger. He could bend their "no" into a "yes" as easy as he could curl a string.

The last straw came when Jimmy turned nine. He announced that he deserved a bigger dirt bike.

"All my friends have big bikes, and I want one, too," he told his parents in a rude sort of way.

"Absolutely not," his mother said.

"Wait until you're thirteen," his father said.

"Thirteen?!" Jimmy cried.

"You need to appreciate what you've got," said his mother.

But he cried bigger than ever and threw a gargantuan fit. So, they bought him the bike—which he wrecked two days later and broke his arm.

It could have been much worse. That night when they returned from the hospital, Jimmy's parents read a few special verses from the book of Proverbs in the Bible, and they had a little talk.

"We should have never bought that dirt bike," said his father.

"We should have trusted our judgment," said his mother.

Jimmy said the next morning at breakfast.

Spoken firmly and in unison, the word could not be mistaken.

Surprise washed the rude expression from Jimmy's face.

"Enough is enough," his father continued.

"Do you see this banana?" His mother's eyes were
big as she held out the dark brown fruit.

"It's bad," Jimmy said, shielding his mouth from some fruit flies.

"Yes," she agreed. "It is spoiled rotten. Can you imagine eating this?"

"No way," he said.

"That banana reminds us of your behavior, son," his father said, gently.

Jimmy was quiet.

"It is spoiled because we ignored it. Now this banana
is past the time to be enjoyed. And, Jimmy, it is past
the time for you to take *no* for an answer.

Crying like a two-year-old when you don't get your way
is not appropriate behavior for a nine-year-old. And
always changing our *no* into a *yes* is bad parenting."

"From now on," his mother said, "*No* means *no.*"

Jimmy pouted all day and long into the night. He wanted a four-wheeler. He and Chad could have a lot of fun on a four-wheeler.

Then he remembered that Chad was not his friend anymore—ever since the day Chad would not share his new remote-controlled helicopter. Jimmy had gotten so angry that he had thrown a fit and smashed Chad's miniature garage.

No more best friend.

Then Jimmy thought about his used-to-be friend Amy,
who would not let him up in line one day last fall. He had
called her a mean name. No more smiles from Amy.

The last thought Jimmy had before he fell asleep was of his parents
and how sad they had looked when they had kissed him goodnight.

He realized that his spoiled rotten behavior
had ruined some good relationships.

His parents were right. It was time to grow up.

Jimmy's mother and father were proud of his decision. Fortunately, if he ever forgot, there were always enough bananas around to remind him!

Proverbs for Parenting

My son, do not despise the LORD's discipline
and do not resent his rebuke,
because the LORD disciplines those he loves,
as a father the son he delights in. 3:11-12

Discipline your son, for in that there is hope;
do not be a willing party to his death. 19:18

Train up a child in the way he should go,
And when he is old he will not depart from it. 22:6 (NKJV)

The rod of correction imparts wisdom,
but a child left to himself disgraces his mother...
Discipline your son, and he will give you peace;
he will bring delight to your soul. 29:15, 17

New Testament Verse

No discipline seems pleasant at the time, but painful. Later on, however, it produces a harvest of righteousness and peace for those who have been trained by it. Hebrews 12:11

Author's Note

Dear Parents and Children,

Thank you for reading *Little Jimmy and the Spoiled Rotten Banana*. This is the first story in my Proverbial Kids series, featuring delightful children in teachable moments. In his Old Testament Commentary on Proverbs, Max Anders writes, "There is no place for a passive parent, particularly in the early years when harmful attitudes have not become hardened patterns. Early correction holds high hope for success."[*]

Toddlers thrive in loving settings of instruction and boundaries, in which the words Yes and No are firm. In today's busy, fast-paced culture, parents often neglect the first stage of discipline, which is *instruction*.

The book of Proverbs is a gold mine of God's wisdom & instruction for every practical area of life—giving and receiving discipline, establishing and adhering to boundaries, work and money ethic, relationship issues, guarding the tongue, and more.

What a delight it is to base my next two stories on a couple of these themes: *Captain Curious and the Invisible Boundary Line*, and *Look-at-Me Lucy and the Rearview Mirror*. I pray this series fortifies your home!

In Christ,

Karen H.

[*] Anders, Max. Holman Old Testament Commentary: Proverbs. Nashville: B&H Publishing Group, 2005. Used by permission, all rights reserved.

Printed in the United States
By Bookmasters